AWKWARD ROMANCE

A Nerdy Girl's Dating Manifesto

Emily Rassam

ISBN-13: 979-8-9913158-1-4 (Print)
ISBN-13: 979-8-9913158-0-7 (Ebook)
LCCN: 2024916546

Cover design by: Emily Rassam

Printed in the United States of America

This dedication is for those who march to the beat of their own drum, the visionaries, and the achievers, past, present, and future, shaping a brighter world. Find joy in laughter and glean wisdom on your journey. Remember, you're not on this path alone! A heartfelt appreciation to my husband, your unwavering support has been my cornerstone. I couldn't have reached this point without you.

CONTENTS

PREFACE

Hey there, fellow awkward adventurer!

I've poured my heart and soul into this book; let me tell you, it's not your typical read. This isn't just a collection of words—it's a journey, an adventure waiting to unfold. I've written these pages with one goal: to ignite a fire within you, shake you from your slumber, and propel you into a life of excitement and possibility.

Life is short, my friend, and it's time we started living like it. From the bustling streets of Pennsylvania to the sun-soaked shores of Florida, the rugged terrain of Tennessee, and the glamorous allure of California—I've traversed them all. Now, I'm here to share my tales of adventure with you.

But this book isn't just about me—it's about you, too. It's about embracing the thrill of the unknown, seizing every opportunity with both hands and living life to the fullest. Ernest Nightingale once said, "We are all self-made, but only the successful will admit it." Let's write our own success stories together, shall we?

So open this book, my friend, and let the adventure begin. Trust me, you won't want to miss a single page. And remember, beauty isn't just about what you see in the mirror—it's about how you live your life, treat others, and embrace every moment with gusto.

So here's to you, me, and the incredible journey ahead. Let's make every moment count.

With love and excitement,

Emily Rassam

THE END

For future reference, if you find yourself in a situation where the man you're dating leisurely crafts peanut butter and jelly sandwiches on the couch, resembling a beached mermaid, heed my advice: run away and do it swiftly!

A wise woman once told me to write the ending to my story before it happened because thoughts and words become reality. Here's some of the nonsense I came up with within my head. It was a beautiful October morning with clear skies and gorgeous rays of sunshine hitting the leaves in the trees, bouncing off in radiant green hues against the backdrop of the warm morning sun rising over the mountains in Southern California. I took off work to enjoy the day outside because it was finally starting to cool down for the fall season. I planned to have breakfast and then go running on the mountain trails. I headed off to the acai place in my new black leggings, sporty t-shirt, baseball cap, and Camelback, much like the usual. But this day was somehow different. I had a date, a date with destiny. It isn't often that you randomly bump into your soul mate, but today was the day. The beauty was it was just an ordinary day. Unfortunately, this isn't how it happened to me. It wasn't that easy, but it's an excellent start for a book about Awkward Romance.

Now for the real story... Sometimes, life gets tough. By tough, I mean it knockdown, drag-out, hits you square in the face with a sucker punch straight out of hell. You are suddenly transformed, like it or not, into someone you never dreamed of. You make a drastic change in your current situation and get this bright idea to move the entire way across a continent to pursue a new career and life, and you can only take what fits in your car because you're determined to enjoy that next fresh start. No matter how much we resist, life has a funny way of creeping up on you, changing you, and taking you places you've never imagined in your wildest dreams. I tell this story to inspire you, dear reader, to follow your bliss. Live a little! Things may not always work out the way you'd expect, but they always work out, eventually, in some way, shape, or form. You probably won't arrive at your destination looking fresh like when you first began your journey. You will, however, inevitably arrive. Life is about the journey, taking action, and pushing forward even when you can't see the entire road ahead. Have the faith to keep moving toward your goals and dreams.

There was a moment when it became crystal clear that it was time to change my life drastically. Maybe it was the soul-sapping, gut-wrenching feeling I got every morning on the way to work or the story I wrote while at the office, comparing it metaphorically to a prison camp. I still have that text and review it every once in a while when I'm feeling stuck. It sure felt like being in prison. Maybe it was my relationship. Perhaps it was me. To solve the problem, like any genuine, certifiably crazy person, I struck out on a new adventure with trepidation, but somehow, everything ended up falling into place. This trepidation phase was a pizza craving-induced heartburn-filled blur that transformed me into what I affectionately call the human volcano. I was so stressed I made myself physically sick; I was unhappy, as evidenced in all of the awful sad face pictures I have of myself from that time.

I dated someone for seven years and was engaged for almost 2, with no commitments. When you start dating someone around the ripe old age of 18, or any age for that matter, you expect them to change and grow over time. Some of us get stuck in our rut and stay the same along with the person we're together with. Relationships are every bit a two-way street, so don't think I'm the innocent one here. You often reach a point where it becomes necessary to rip off the Band-Aid. It would be best to do intense relationship counseling; pray a miracle will happen or you will have to change. It's okay; all of us change at different rates, and it's not always that you're with a bad person or that they won't change down the road. Still, you may be at a different point in your life; the person may be feeling bad about themselves, or they just aren't ever going to make a change because it's not part of their life path. Change takes work. It's hard—no judgment toward anyone who isn't ready to change coming from me.

Many of us get into relationships thinking we will change someone and help them with some insurmountable difficulty they face. Some magic happens, and everything becomes a happily-ever-after fairy tale story. Please learn from my experience; that is why I wrote this book, and if you can, share it with someone you love who might need to hear the story. Everyone needs to listen to this story; I wish someone had told it to me sooner. But you know, we all hear what we need to hear when we are ready to listen.

At times, we find ourselves at a crossroads where commitment becomes a crucial decision. It's important to recognize when the person you're with isn't the right fit. I'm sharing my story and putting it all on the line because I don't want people to go through the same situation I did or the same difficulties my fiance experienced. Even if you're in the weeds right now, there's hope. It is terrible for you to stay with the person you need to let go of, and sometimes it's bad for that person, too; parting ways may be just the thing you both need to grow and have the best lives possible. It's tough, don't get me wrong, breaking up if you've been dating for a long time is the pits. It isn't easy financially. It's tricky dating again because you feel guilty. You feel awkward after not kissing another person in 7 years. You may even feel like you're cheating after the breakup. If you're talking to a loved one you think is in the same situation, I suggest that they sit down and take an hour to think about how their life will be in 5 or 10 years with the person they're dating now. If this is you, use your head before serving real damage to your significant other.

Do you see yourself becoming a power couple? See yourself being stuck? Do you see good things or bad things coming your way? People can change, but change isn't for everyone; it's difficult and scary, and sometimes parting ways is the best gift you can give someone you love. When you go through something difficult, it often inspires both of you to get your shit together. I secretly checked up on my ex over the years, and he had accomplished all the goals he talked about when we were together. Do you know how good that makes you feel? It's justification for the crappy stuff you both had to go through; honestly, it makes me so proud. I am happy for him and his family. Don't think being the bad guy occasionally is wrong; our parents must do it for us as kids. When you become an adult, you have to do it for yourself; you have to do it for those you love, even if it is challenging and makes you upset.

Congratulations if you picture yourself 5 or 10 years from now and see your significant other in the picture. For some of us, that takes decades to achieve. We are proud of you and wish you all the best. I am not advocating divorce. Sometimes, it is even necessary for one's safety to divorce. I am not downplaying abusive relationships, and I am not encouraging couples who don't always see eye to eye to end things because they disagree. I chose to end my relationship because I knew in my heart that I could not promise my fiance that I would be with him for the rest of our lives had we married. There was an awful feeling in the pit of my stomach when I visualized saying, "Till death do us part." Promises are sacred to me, and I take them extremely seriously.

ROMANTIC HONEYMOON FOR ONE

Sometimes God (or the universe, if you are so inclined) has this divine way of sending a stranger into your life that you semi-spill your guts out to, and they have no attachment to you whatsoever. Still, they give you an honest opinion of what you should do with your life. That's what happened to me.

When you run into someone who has been in your shoes before, and they ask you what's going on and if you are okay, and you say you are so stressed because this thing happened to you, It has to do with the person I'm dating, and I don't know what to do. Then that mystery person says, "I've been in that situation; it sounds to me like you're an amazing person, and you need to make a change for both of you for both of your sake so that you can both grow and be the people you're supposed to be." Push comes to shove. A wedding may or may not have been canceled two weeks before the - I do. Thank you, random stranger, you saved my ass! Celebrate anyway, postpone your honeymoon, go alone, and live the dream.

If you do happen to visit your family members who were planning to come in for your wedding on your supposed wedding week, it will be awkward. It's still a big surprise to them, especially when you feel you've been over it for a long time. Some brave souls will say they're proud of you for doing something challenging; that feels pretty amazing. Others will treat you like you have the plague and don't know what to say; that's okay, too. They're breathing along with you. Everyone takes awkward situations in different ways. Don't get upset; you will have to face reality at some point. Might as well do it quickly. On to the honeymoon!

There I was, sitting at a pub on the water, alone in Martha's Vineyard near Edgartown, Massachusetts, on what was supposed to be my honeymoon trip, plotting my next moves over a pint of Stella Artois and a world-famous lobster roll. For those unfamiliar with the Vineyard, it's chilly, even in the summer months, so the beer was warming and well-received. Sometimes, life happens. Life happens big time. You're scared half to death, running on fumes and ambitions, with only your life goals and divine purpose carrying you forward. Don't be afraid as someone with a vast array of hands-on experience. Good things come from high-pressure and stressful situations. Those are the times in which you grow the most. Hello, diamonds and pearls. Those are supposed to be a woman's best friend, perhaps for good reason.

Traveling alone can be tricky the first time, but I've found that after you push yourself through the gut-wrenching feelings of self-doubt and fear, you can grow into your skin by being out of your comfort zone—some of the best adventures I have experienced were when I've gone to new places alone. Once, I ended up at a bar and met some guy who supposedly made guitars for Aerosmith; then I had to duck out and pretend I was going to the bathroom but leave because insert creeper story here. Or the time I went out with friends to a random Southern California country club and ended up behind the stage with the guys who owned the place, counting all the cash and eating Twizzlers. The time I sat down at breakfast with a friend and then ended up in Mexico one hour later drinking tequila on the beach while working next to the border fence so I could still get internet from the US. Then there's my favorite story about when my now-husband took me out for a Syrian dinner for the first time. After our date, I called my dad. I told him I was the sluttiest girl in the restaurant; for reference, I was wearing something that I would typically wear to church, but when everybody else is wearing burkas - good luck trying to blend in wearing a dress that goes down to your knees.

When you travel alone, you meet people you'd never talk to if you were traveling with a significant other or a group of friends. Often, people will talk to you because you "look cool" or have something in common with them. One of the best things about traveling is that you usually know no one and can be yourself without inhibition. You can be someone you may never share with your family and friends because responsibilities bog you down while working and taking care of your home and family. If you've ever hiked alone, you know what I'm talking about. Once in a while, you'll meet up with people on the trail just because you're heading in the same direction, talk about life, and part ways. Connecting with random strangers, just for a time, is one of those things that life is all about.

The best way to promote self-awareness and growth is to get out of your comfort zone frequently. When things go wrong, and you feel uncomfortable, you will feel awkward, shocking your system into growing. One weekend, my now husband and I taught ourselves to ski while on vacation in Alta, Utah. Please note that I am not encouraging you to do dangerous things without instruction. Going for it is one way to get out of your comfort zone. Who cares if you mess up!? We were hiking in giant snow drifts, without snowshoes, sinking into feet of snow, when we suddenly decided to go skiing. My husband was wearing shorts, and I was wearing yoga pants. So we rented skis and spent hours on the bunny slopes having a grand time falling, freezing, and busting our butts rather gracefully. Give yourself permission to try new things and fail. Be the you that you want to live vicariously through. You might have some fun along the way.

LIVING VICARIOUSLY

L et's face it; we all want to be that friend or Instagram-famous person everyone is living life vicariously through. That friend that takes those romantic trips with their ultra-sexy significant other to luxurious and often remote tropical destinations goes sky-diving on a random Wednesday afternoon and takes their yacht to Bora Bora because it's a glorious Tuesday. We all secretly hate that friend but, strangely, can't stop spending time with them, or at least checking in secretly, hoping that some of their mojo rubs off on us and we end up looking like those super sexy models in swimsuits everyone raves about. The common denominator here is persistence, but we often need more time and focus to see things happening before our eyes. Crafting and charting the course of your life requires unwavering perseverance, a pivotal motif woven seamlessly throughout this entire manuscript.

The saying goes, "A journey of 1,000 miles begins with a single step."

–Unknown

Allow me to indulge my nerdy side and delve into some simple math. The average stride length for a human is approximately 2.5 feet. Let's simplify things by considering there are 2,000 steps in one mile. So, if we multiply 2,000 steps by 1,000 miles, we arrive at roughly 2 million steps. Thus, your journey of 1,000 miles comprises approximately 2 million individual steps. Fortunately, you are the one who determines how many single steps you take at a time, the speed, and the direction. You choose how quickly you complete your journey and where you end up. Success is achieved through persistence, not speed, strength, or intelligence.

For many years, one of my goals was to live the life others want to live vicariously through. For a while, I thought that goal was somewhat selfish. Being an American and living in a free country has already given me and countless others more opportunities than we deserve. So many people have given their lives to pursue freedom and opportunity. The pursuit of living the "American Dream." We owe it to our fellow humans to recognize our freedoms and use them to improve the world, our lives, and our families daily. Today, I'm thankful to be a boring old housewife accomplishing goals, persistently. In February 2022, the world woke up to the horrors of the Russian government sending troops to take over Ukraine. It has been wholly inspiring and heartbreaking to millions over the world to see the Ukrainian people clinging to their freedom and standing up for their convictions. As I write this, we don't yet know the outcome of this war. Their only path is forward. It was a passionate reminder for me that if we focus all our energy on something we want to achieve, there is no way to fail. Despite setbacks and distractions, it's essential to relentlessly pursue your passions, goals, and dreams.

Let me clarify—I still find joy in traveling with my family to the Islands or venturing off to remote locations. I fully intend to embrace all the experiences life has to offer. Sneaking off to Mexico with your closest friend to work remotely while lounging on the beach remains a fantastic adventure, one I've had the pleasure of enjoying. I've also embarked on spontaneous journeys, like driving halfway across the country in the dead of night. From boating in the Islands to backpacking through Europe, from sleeping on a train station bench to indulging in five-star hotels and fancy cars—I've savored it all, especially clad in my favorite red lipstick. Living your best life shouldn't induce guilt; it's a tribute to those who haven't yet realized the splendor life holds when you dare to take risks and embrace sleepless nights, early mornings, and wild escapades. Your best life isn't always found in clandestine getaways; sometimes, it's in the simple routines and everyday moments that bring the greatest fulfillment.

I recently went out for breakfast. Typically, when we do family things, I try to forget my cell phone at home or only take it for pictures. I've developed the habit of wearing a traditional analog watch. Not only does it add a touch of sophistication to my appearance, but it also helps me avoid the distractions of cell phones and wearable devices. As we sat playing together in our booth, we looked around to see that almost every table had people sitting there. Begin by setting aside your cell phone and switching off your television (or any other distractions that resonate with you). You'll find yourself with plenty of additional time, believe me. By disconnecting, you'll not only reclaim the time spent in those activities but also gain the freedom from worrying about things beyond your control. Managing our screen time is a skill we could all improve upon, and I'm committed to urging you to set aside your devices and engage in face-to-face interactions. Whether it's for a simple coffee catch-up or a phone call to hear their voice, these moments are magical and foster deeper, more meaningful connections. Please, do yourself a favor and take a moment to zip your purse shut and resist the urge to constantly check your phone. If you find it challenging to engage in meaningful conversations, take the opportunity to practice and improve your skills.

CHAOS UNLEASHED

There's something about venturing solo that sends shivers down the spine of the average individual, particularly older family members. Those who love and care about you often become your most vocal critics, hindering you from pursuing worthwhile adventures. Fear, that primal instinct honed over millennia, is a construct of the mind. The way you see yourself and your life can steer the ship of your existence. So, if you want to sail through smooth waters, maybe sprinkle in a bit of optimism and a pinch of humor along the way! This invaluable lesson was imparted to me by a friend, a former marine, during a hike near a breathtaking waterfall. The water thundered as it cascaded over the falls, a familiar symphony heard at the base of most grand waterfalls. My boots were soaked and slippery, and the only way to get across quickly was to jump between two river rocks nearly 2 meters apart (6 feet for our American Friends). River rocks pose a slippery and potentially hazardous challenge, for those unfamiliar with hiking. Being a showoff, Mr. Jarhead quickly jumped between the rocks and over the fast-moving water beneath us.

On the other hand, I was seriously concerned about slipping, as a 6-foot jump is not my forte, even on the dry ground. Yelling down to me from way up the hill, Mr. Jarhead said, **"It's all in your head; just know you're going to make it across, and you will."** Not being one to back down from a challenge, I finally did jump, made it across, soaked my wet boots even more, and hastily marched up the hill with my head held high. Imagine my surprise as I proceeded to ascend the seemingly innocuous staircase, only to discover myself engulfed in a surreal hue of blue, with my hands, feet, and lips succumbing to an alarming case of cyanosis. Yes, in my infinite wisdom, I deemed it a brilliant notion to sprint up the roughly 1,100 steps to reach the summit. Oh, the charm of it all! Only later did I learn that caution served me well in my jump across the rocks as Mr. Jarhead severely bruised his ankle. Bonus points to me for taking a more calculated risk than Mr. Jarhead.

You don't ever get over having that awful feeling in the pit of your stomach when you're taking risks; it's that you keep on marching onward and upward despite the dreadful feelings. You take risks and chances without looking back or worrying about a pair of wet socks, or even a little bit of severe cyanosis. The good news for the naysayers is that the more risks you take, the easier it gets and the better your lung capacity gets. Opportunities never arise when you think you're ready for them; they come up when you least expect them. The tricky part is feeding them and making them seem so close in your mind that you take the opportunities even though they're inconvenient and cause you to lose plenty of sleep at night.

The gravest risks are the ones avoided—missed connections and declined adventures due to weariness. Amidst fatigue, greatness emerges. Timing will never be perfect; perseverance through adversity is key. Embrace change; true happiness emanates from within, transcending circumstances. A few of the stupid risks I've taken include not following my skill set and wasting time getting an education for something I never ended up using, listening too much to other people's opinions, and even wasting time watching television in the past. There's nothing like realizing that you have wasted some of the best years of your life watching television instead of climbing mountains or seeking a new business venture. The biggest risk of all is wanting something so badly and not taking action to accomplish the thing you want. The worst thing you can have happen is that some people will tell you no. If you want that something badly enough, go for it and figure it out along the way!

Some of the best risks I've taken include marrying my husband, whom I had been dating for a mere 11 months, jumping out of airplanes, traveling the world, trying in business and failing, trying in business and succeeding, and allowing myself to find love. Finding love is scary! It's not for the faint of heart to allow yourself to be vulnerable with someone.

The worst risks are the ones you are too afraid to take. The connections you were too tired to make. The adventures you turned down because you were exhausted. As I embrace my 30s, I've come to the conclusion that you will be exhausted at times, but you know what? Some of the best things in life come about when you're off your ass exhausted, but you keep going anyway. There is never an ideal time to accomplish your goals; you must push through the pain, exhaustion, and stress to achieve them. It's not easy, but someone has to realize your goals, and that person is you. Keep going, work on the things you find in your heart, pursue them relentlessly.

Embrace change, learn to love change, and you will go far. Money, fame, love, and happiness come and go. True joy is from within and you can retrieve it in even the worst situations and the most embarrassing ones. That's something I've had to remind myself of a lot lately. Especially now that I'm a married mother of three. Embrace new people in your community; remember that you are the ambassador for your own unique part of the world.

Life is an adventure full of unexpected twists and turns. You never know when new opportunities and people will come across your path and change the game plan. You think your course is carved in stone sometimes. Then, you're sent off in an entirely new direction when a person or an opportunity appears. These are the times when you discover just how tough you genuinely are. The gifts and talents you've developed along the way are fantastic.

It truly is "all in your head." Whether a 6 ft leap overflowing water on slippery river rocks, asking someone on a date, or a new business you're considering starting. Take a calculated risk, crunch the numbers, and ask yourself if the risk is propelling you toward your goal.

The gnawing sensation in the pit of your stomach persists when taking risks; the key is to press onward despite the dread. With each risk embraced, opportunities multiply. They seldom align with our readiness but emerge unexpectedly, demanding our attention despite inconvenience and sleepless nights.

BREAKING FREE

At some point, I got the crazy idea to move to California with no job and no place to live. So, of course... I decided selling insurance to get paid to meet new people for work was a great idea. Three weeks later, I was a licensed property and casualty agent with a place to live. The first apartment I went to ended up being "the one." Not going to lie, you have a few oh no moments in those situations, but somehow it all works out.

The day I left for California, there was a total solar eclipse. I set out from South Georgia to Tallahassee, Florida, where my alma mater, Florida State University, is located, to meet a friend for lunch. Everyone was panicking about the solar eclipse and worried about me driving and getting out of town before the total eclipse happened. I left town around 1 pm and was halfway to Panama City on I-10 when the eclipse occurred. When it started getting dark midday, I pulled over at a roadside rest stop. I made some eclipse glasses with some toilet paper and a pair of reflective oversized cat eye quay sunglasses, Macguiver style. That night, I drove to Southern Louisiana, stopped for a bite to eat in New Orleans, and then pulled over for a quick nap at a 24-hour store before heading to Shreveport for a workout and shower at the gym, true gypsy style. The following night, next was Wichita Falls, Texas. It turns out my brother worked at a nightclub there for a while back in his 20s—small freaking world. The next day, I traveled through Amarillo, TX. I sang along to some of my favorite classic country songs while heading for Albuquerque, NM. In case you were wondering, I didn't take a wrong left turn once I arrived. Hello, awkward cultural references (please look this up if you don't get the connection). It was my first time in New Mexico, and it was quite a hot summer. My stuffed-to-the-gill four-door Fiat had a bicycle on the back. Man, was I cool.

By freak accident, I traveled to Sedona, Arizona, because the four-star resort was incredibly cheap. I was on the phone with one of my best friends, driving from Flagstaff down to Sedona, when I saw this beautiful desert scenery. In my mind, it never clicked that it was the Sedona that many people enjoy visiting for romantic getaways with the red rocks. I accidentally stayed in Sedona, which turned out to be quite beautiful. I remember it like it was yesterday, I was driving in the car and telling my best friend, "Oh wow, Sedona is nice." That was quite a significant blonde moment, of which I've had many in my day, but it was unforgettable. I can't wait to visit again. The scenery was beautiful and romantic. I thought, "I can't wait to go there with my significant other in the future."

The biggest obstacle in any endeavor is fighting back against your mind. Nothing can throw you roadblocks and speed bumps faster than not having faith and listening to your critics. The biggest ones are typically your family and loved ones. Take it from an expert. I have received some of the worst advice in my entire life from the people I love the most. My advice is, just don't ask. Pray about it. Keep your mind from telling you you're too tired to do things. This little sneaking issue will creep up on all your hopes and dreams; go for it (whatever "it" is). Some of the best parts of my life have happened while I was broke and flat-out exhausted. Hello, backpacking through Europe, late-night college adventures, hiking, and becoming a parent.

About faith, it is something that all of us possess. The world has a way of convincing you to give up on those things you hold in your heart. More of us need to wake up and follow through with faith. Whether or not you are religious, It is a necessity in your arsenal; all of us feel that spiritual tug. Sometimes, you think in your mind that you shouldn't go somewhere, so you skip it and find out you missed a massive accident. I remind myself every time that I am running late for something of the people who lost their lives in the tragic events of September 11, 2001, and of the people whose lives were saved because they were either running late, missed a flight, or slept in. Embrace where you are at any given time, and don't stress when you are running late; maybe it is for a good reason. We're all where we are supposed to be at any given time. Sometimes we're there to learn a lesson where we're getting bitten in the butt, and it's painful, or we're there to bless others, or there to save our life.

IN THE MIDDLE OF NOWHERE

As I write this, I sit under the stars in Jean, Nevada. The sky is so big out here. It is so vast it makes all your problems seem small. Bats are squeaking and fluttering about, little red Farmall tractors are plowing the dry, dusty earth, and the sound of children and families abound. It starkly contrasts nearby Las Vegas, the crowds, the prices, the merchandise, and the people. Out here, you feel a sense of peace, as if you're part of the earth and belong. As the sun sinks below the Spring Mountain Range near Devil's Peak, the sky turns from blue to pink, orange, yellow, and finally, the deep violet hue of nighttime. Slowly, the crickets begin to chirp. You feel the ever-present smell of dry and dusty earth in your nostrils, like having a piece of chalk shoved up your nose for hours straight. I cannot wait to see the stars come out in stark contrast to the cold night sky. Being in an isolated place in the middle of nowhere has a way of making you feel small. It's similar to waiting in the interminable line at the California DMV but much more breath-taking and inspirational. Planes flying from Las Vegas soar over the mountains, passing by the areas where time moves slowly, the flyover spaces. Time, after all, is relative.

During my time in Jean, I met some of the craziest misfits and desert dust-covered humans a person could ever come across. These are the people most don't even notice except when you see them, and they look out of place. But suppose you've ever genuinely been in a bind, and so broke that you live off dried beans you've purchased in bulk to save money. In that case, you'd realize that even though these people may not have anything, they are some of the most caring and giving people you will ever meet. I recently read Benjamin Franklin's autobiography and came to appreciate the necessity of the forced vegetarian diet. Benjamin Franklin was a founding father and, aside from being a scallywag, was so frugal throughout his young adult life that he often scrimped, saved, and talked others into strictly budgeting their food expenditures. Benjamin was a scientist, a politician, a writer, a businessman, and a printer, which drew me to him in the first place. I've tried a little of everything in my day and, somewhere along the way, got tired of living the dull life some people think they must follow. However, after later research on Benjamin, I realized that it was really his wife who helped him keep his life together. Teamwork, makes the dream work.

There have been many times when I was sticking to a strict budget and could only buy "dollar store gourmet," as I have affectionately termed those broke and only eating bean diets. However, I did not write about this as extensively as Benjamin Franklin. I don't know where you are in life, but I do know that eating healthy to the best of your ability is good for your mind, body, and soul. It can be hard to make wise choices when you are on a budget, but beans are pretty good and cheap. If you're on the "dollar store gourmet" diet, never fear; there is hope at the end of the long winter: spring will come. One of the most essential life skills is mental fitness; it can get you through the most challenging times and bring you out the other side, shining and bright. It can mean the difference between giving up or conquering your fears and goals like a champion. Whether those goals involve love, career, finance, family, or faith.

When you're surrounded by miles of nothing, in my experience, one of the best places to think, meditate, and listen to what God or the universe has to say to you. Without this solitude, it can be overwhelmingly challenging to sit and listen. Over the years, I've had the most breakthroughs when surrounded by nothing but nature, no matter what kind. In those times, you learn to appreciate the necessities. In the desert, you learn the importance of water; in the forest, you learn the importance of staying dry from the rain and mists. In the river, you learn the importance of dry boots. Climbing hills, you learn the importance of breathing and cardio, which you don't think you need when you're comfy on the couch. Getting out of your comfort zone is important to help you learn where you are lacking.

When leaving for an adventure, the necessities are the best preparations you can make. The most valuable things in life are faith, the company you keep, and the experiences you share with others. Love is what it's all about. You would be surprised where creativity, curiosity, and tenacity can take you. These are all gifts that each of us possess. Every day is an adventure; prepare accordingly! The stuff and things don't matter so much.

SOURCES OF INSPIRATION

When you're driving through the desert, see all the bushes in front of you littering the landscape with no real trees. Somewhere in the middle of the Arizona desert, I came up with the title of this book. Toward the end of my first solo East-West, cross-country driving trip, I was getting a bit crazy. For entertainment, I was thinking of greeting card ideas and saw some tumbleweed and some bushes on the side of the road. The card I imagined was for a long-distance relationship; the picture on the front would be a person standing behind or beside a bush planted in their yard and saying, "My bush has grown so much since I last saw you." Awkward!! And, there you have it... the title for this book.

Sometimes, you find inspiration in desolate locations. My best ideas have often come from doing the most mundane tasks and sheer boredom. As we age, we usually find it more and more challenging to experience boredom. Being discontent with the status quo also helps inspire you to become a better person. It's not that you don't appreciate every moment in life; you know there is more out there, so you get the bright idea to force yourself to improve. You think outside the box to come up with new and revolutionary ideas. You start a "self-revolution" and unabashedly pursue your dreams while changing yourself along the way.

"Life isn't about finding yourself. Life is about creating yourself."

–Unknown.

We're all as strong, innovative, and talented as our imaginations can grasp. Fortunately, with a little effort, you, too, can learn to use your imagination again. Think of it as reverse-adulting. Don't be afraid to have crazy ideas, to be creative, and to practice using your imagination daily. Ask many questions about something you are curious about just because it gives you joy. Read fewer books and do more interviews.

"Go confidently in the direction of your dreams! Live the life you've imagined."

– Thoreau

Sometimes inspiration comes from people you've just met, a new friend who instantly tells you you're good at something. Often, you get the best advice from strangers because these people have no real attachment to you, don't feel interconnected with your well-being, and are not emotionally attached to you like family. Today, I learned from someone that I am well-versed in food and nutrition. My colleague recommended that I develop a great nutrition plan, follow it, and document my adventure to inspire others. It was quite an excellent idea, and I have considered pursuing it with great enthusiasm. **Always be prepared for inspiration because it's often when you least expect it that inspiration strikes.** It didn't make financial sense to me then, so I filed it to my list of ideas for later review.

There are many phrases out there that describe the opportunity.
One of my favorites is, "When one door closes, another opens."
– Unknown.

Sure, another door may have opened, but were you ready for it? You must be prepared for changes so you can go with your shoes laced and backpack on and jump when an opportunity arises. Embrace the power of change; don't run from it. One of the best ways to ensure you're ready for the option is to focus on becoming personal debt-free (not the same as business debt). When you owe money, you do not have the freedom to make drastic changes in your life. We've all been on that dollar-store gourmet diet at one point or another. Don't make that your staple. Onward and upward!

Today truly is the first day of the rest of your life. Embrace this opportunity to make meaningful connections and extend a helping hand to those in need. Consider volunteering your time and energy to causes that resonate with you. Engage in physical activities like sports to invigorate your body and mind, or seek a stunning view to refresh your spirit. Savor the simple pleasures, whether enjoying a warm cup of tea or spending time at your favorite café. Every moment holds the potential for new experiences and joy.

Listen to that little voice inside you; it often knows the way. Rarely does it lead you astray. Trusting your inner guidance can open doors to unexpected adventures and profound satisfaction. Whether you find solace in nature, community service, or personal hobbies, following your instincts can lead to a more prosperous, more fulfilling life. Make the most of today, and let your intuition guide you where you need to be.

A STRONG FOUNDATION

There's something about being so broke you can't afford anything that doesn't come from the dollar store dried beans section or selling everything you own that teaches you the value of what matters in life. Yes, it's nice to enjoy life's little luxuries, but in the long run, they don't mean nearly as much as the experiences you have. I, for one, always told myself that when I could afford to eat berries for breakfast on the regular, and not the frozen ones either, then I'd know I was living a life of luxury.

People spend their entire lives chasing after feelings they think they'll have when they achieve their vision. In the end, do things matter? Some people would call this point "rock bottom." Although, it never really felt that way to me. It was an adventure and worth every freaking stress-filled moment. In my mind, I was out discovering a whole new world, learning, growing, and exploring.

Don't get me wrong. Living in abject poverty does have a way of motivating you to get your butt in gear and start getting creative with finding ways to make money, ways to have fun, and ways to fake it until you make it. One of my absolute favorite things to do was to visit all the most luxurious hotels I could find and order a cup of coffee. I've read that many people do this on their rise to the top, and part of me understands why. It also made me realize I wasn't the only crazy person visiting luxurious locations for cups of coffee and incredible views. In these situations, you know that even when you do not have a lot, you can still truly enjoy the finer things in life, even when you have to go home and eat a whole cup of beans with taco seasoning because you can't afford anything else.

Never let yourself feel less of a person because you're not yet where you want to be. Inconveniences are part of the journey and sure as hell teach you gratitude. I remember the first time my now husband put air in my car tires for me. I felt like a million bucks. It even secretly made me cry that someone would do that for me. Sometimes, when you're broke, for a while, you start to think of yourself as less of a human who is undeserving of love. Society is constantly bombarding us with this idea of the picture-perfect lifestyle we're supposed to live. Secretly, no one lives a picture-perfect life; it's a complete and utter lie but also quite motivational. No one lives in sunshine and rainbows every single day. I don't care who you are; there will be days when you are less than enthused, tired, or even anxious. Downturns are part of life and make the good times even more extraordinary. Take time for gratitude daily, and you'll realize there are many opportunities to be thankful.

Do whatever it takes to reach your perceived level of success. It doesn't matter where you come from, your career, ethnicity, or your parents! Going from nothing to something in life is challenging but doable.

LETTING GO

When I moved to California from Tennessee, I learned a lot of new vocabulary. There was the first time someone told me I was "bitchin" in SoCal (Southern California, for those not familiar with the term). It turns out that means you're cool, but in Southern Slang, you're complaining annoyingly. As in "stop your bitchin." When I started meeting people, they were constantly impressed that somehow, as a woman, I drove there from the tip of Florida to Southern California to create a new life myself. Add being a scientist and business graduate into the mix, and people are 100% not sure what to say. Sometimes, I like to make up unrealistic stats, just like many news journals do, to drive home my points. The best conversations go something like this:

New Person- "What type of scientist are you?"

You- "A mycologist and microbiologist with degrees in Biology, Chemistry, and Biomedical Physics."

New Person- "Oh, Microbiology. I love microbiology. Don't you guys make beer or something?"

You- "Yes, some microbiologists focus on the fermentation of beverages and other consumables."

New Person- "Science fascinates me; I watch it on television constantly." "Isn't physics just so cool; have you heard of Nicola Tesla?" "I just watched a documentary on him."

You - Can't stop thinking they know nothing about science and are trying to sound smart to be impressive. I've heard about this documentary a thousand times.

For those of you naysayers, yes, it is challenging moving to an entirely new area alone. Being alone and away from the normal teaches you one thing: perseverance. You also either learn to communicate with other people effectively, or you end up locked away at home or flying solo everywhere you go when you're away from the office. Family members can be simultaneously your most prominent advocates and your worst enemies when it comes to risk-taking. They feel angst and trepidation for you and force you to be strong and overcome your fears. I encourage you to think of this as a good thing. But also keep some things private. Take a lesson from poker and bluff once in a while. If you can get past the wall of fear your family members unintentionally build in your heart, you can do anything. Anything!

What do you do when you're afraid? Chuck it in the bucket, is my term for suppressing the feelings and moving forward in spite of fear. Allowing fear to keep you in place is like consciously not enjoying a bowl of delicious creamy ice cream because it might be too cold and give you that always-dreaded brain freeze. I'll take mine with sprinkles, please! We all have hang-ups and self-doubt galore. We've all gone through tough times, but remember, this is all relative. One Person's tough time was getting blown up fighting in a war and losing a limb. Another person, such as a toddler, thinks getting a hangnail or burning your tongue on a pop-tart is a rough day.

You see, the theory of relativity doesn't only apply to time and space. It's not rocket science, people. If there's one thing all humans can relate to, it's struggle. It's those "oh no" moments where you have no idea what to do, but somehow, when everything is said and done, you survive despite it all. If you haven't had any of those moments, you're either a zombie or a missing link to alternative life forms. Those "oh shit" moments are the ones that help you grow the most. It's like how, in the army, they quickly try to break you down and make you feel worthless, then get you to problem-solve with your team to increase your confidence. When thinking about your past relationships, please don't fret; think of them as learning experiences. The worse the experience, the more you probably learned about yourself and about what you expect from a significant other in the future.

This military training principle works in dating. The more you focus on making yourself a better person and learning about your unique preferences, the more attractive you become to others with the positive energy you're giving off. When you focus on your spirituality, needs, wants, and desires, you inevitably meet other awesome people. Some of my goals before meeting my fantastic husband were to focus on my health, overcome my many food allergies, finish this book, and plan my next business. Did you know that if you write just 600 words daily, you can have an entire book in only three months? Don't feel bad if it takes you longer, though! I finished this baby up in a quick... five years. One principle for success that has become the most impactful in my life is the Japanese philosophy of kaizen. If you aren't familiar with it, kaizen is a practice where you do more daily until you accomplish your goals and dreams.

For example, I want to be able to do 100 pushups. To accomplish this, I start with seven and add one daily until I'm up to 100 pushups daily. You don't have to push yourself to the breaking point to meet your goals; results stack up over time. While the principle of kaizen is quite helpful in certain situations, goals often need to be accomplished more quickly. In that case, you can make them your "push-it goals." As a recovering scientist, I love to come up with a goal and break it down into days, hours, and minutes. Everything seems more attainable when you don't have to do it all at once.

I learned many of my lessons from the best. My mother always said, "You learn something from everyone in the world; sometimes, it's how not to act and what not to say." Growing up, I spent much time around complainers, and I'm eternally grateful for that. Yes, you heard me. I'm thankful for the tough times I went through growing up. Do you hear many people say that? I don't think so. For one, the best part about growing up around people who weren't content with their situation is that I learned these two valuable lessons. Lesson One: Don't complain about something if you are unwilling to make changes. Lesson Two: If you make changes, you'll have the opportunity to have a different life. When I was a kid, I remember being complained about the most: I didn't have enough money, I never had time to take vacations, and I wouldn't say I liked how I looked in these clothes. In short, I learned that whining is the easy way out. If you're a tough cookie, you "suck it up, buttercup," and go be that person you always dreamed of in the flesh.

While I was dating, I was particularly discontent with three things in my life: I wouldn't say I liked the lifestyle my finances afforded me, I wanted to find an extraordinary significant other (or, as I like to call him, the other half of our power couple), and I wanted to be in better shape. These are three things most everyone can relate to at some point in their life. There's nothing wrong with being discontent! Things go sour when you don't make plans to make the changes necessary to make your thoughts into reality. **Write your dreams down, discuss them with your confidants, and share them with the people you care about the most.** The next step is to break things down into simple steps. Anyone is capable of making gradual, small changes in their life. Nothing big ever happens overnight. Just ask anyone you think of as successful. A lot of blood, sweat, and tears go into making changes in your life. This year, I'm particularly proud of being able to wake up at 5:00 am every day; thanks to our exceptional children, I feel energized throughout the day, and that's a significant help for accomplishing goals and dreams.

Think of it this way. **When you wake up two hours earlier than usual every day for an entire year, you have 2 hours times 365 days; that's an extra 730 hours a year to work on things that aren't related to your day job.** Seven hundred thirty hours divided by 24 hours/day is a full 30 days. If that doesn't blow your mind, then there's something wrong with you. I was inspired to do this math because one day, as I used my toothbrush with a timer, I realized that if I brush my teeth for two minutes twice a day, that's four. Four minutes/day * 7 days/week * 52 weeks/year is 1456 minutes or an entire day of your life. If you multiply that by the average life expectancy, that's almost 1/3 of a year. Crazy right? So, how many days would it be if you got 30 years of waking up two hours earlier?

We're keeping this math simple, so I've done a minor rounding, and it's not going to be the exact number, but 30 days a year for 30 years is about 900 days or about 2.5 years. How's that for an eye-opener? So when people tell you you're crazy for waking up two hours early every day, do this little bit of simple math for them. The statisticians will be upset with my math skills here, but I wanted to keep it simple. If you arrive at work 10 to 15 minutes early every day and have a career lasting 40 years (that's an average). How much time do you waste that you could have spent with your family? Let's say 15 minutes for this case because sometimes you skip lunch or leave work late. That's a full 106 days of your life. So next time you think about those extra few minutes, think of it this way. What are your priorities? Think of this next time you're on your cell phone, sitting around with family. Think of this the next time someone says to you time is money. Think of this every time you're trying to get your priorities straight. Think of this when you're making big work decisions. Work takes up almost 1/3 of your life, so pick the right job, something other than what you hate. Again, the stats people are screaming because I didn't factor in being a kid, being retired, and weekends.

None of us know when our last day will come. So make every moment count. The older I get, the more thankful I am to spend time with family. When you become an adult, "the feels" come in, and you realize that life is short. It's like gambling every day. That's one of the major appeals of being around children. They remind us that we don't always need to take life so seriously. None of us is getting out of here alive. The older I get, the more I cry about things that touch my heart or have a lot of meaning. I used to think that only weak people allowed themselves to cry. Now I know that it's the strong people who share their emotions with others. You never know when you'll see a friend or loved one for the last time, so you learn to hold them tighter and be more understanding. Deep down, I'm convinced that most people are aware of this, but not everyone is willing to admit that they, too, will be six feet under someday.

When you learn how fragile life is, you're willing to take more risks, love deeper, hug a little tighter, jump out of a few more airplanes, and laugh a little more. You're also more likely to work a little wiser and give to others without expecting anything back. So, enough of this morbidity thing; let's talk more about the awkward romance of that nerd woman and the valuable life lessons learned along the way.

DISCOVERING DORY

When I first moved to California, I was experiencing massive amounts of heartburn because my life was drastically changing rapidly. I felt like I didn't have my shit together, and sometimes, from experience, that becomes downright terrifying.

Many people don't know where the author of the book they read was writing and working at the time. So here's the back story. I was being paid to work at the front desk at a hotel and writing while on the clock. It was somewhat of a dream job in a way. I'd probably have been asleep in bed if I hadn't had that job. Instead, I was working toward my dream and getting paid. Not everything you do to reach your goals is glamorous. No one tells you about the countless extra hours, the lack of sleep, and the stress about getting everything else done before you get to writing. Or how sometimes you have to let things slide in your life so you can accomplish your burning desires. A lesson you become further acquainted with if/when you have kids.

On my first day of work at a lovely hotel in Newport Beach, California, I was directly in the middle of trying to find myself. Aside from this, the Inn is a quaint Victorian-era motif bed and breakfast. I didn't even apply for the job, so I took it as a sign that I needed to use the downtime to finish this book so that my readers would benefit from me sharing my life experiences.

By the ripe old age of twenty-eight, I had slowly become one of those women who didn't want to settle down and had moved from place to place, trying new adventures as much as possible. While the thought seems alluring, it's much less glamorous than one might expect. Being that woman may sound like all fun and games, but it often gets quite lonely, and after a while, it starts to scare the men away. Sure, I got to see and experience things many people have always dreamed about doing, but I also missed out on family time, and the precious moments so many of the loved ones in my life were experiencing. I may have found Dory, but what had I lost?

No matter where you are, remember the grass is always greener on the other side. **Remember to be content with where you are, but never settle or stop making changes and improvements.** On a positive note, the hotel business gave me extra time to resume writing this book. Being an author was a dream I'd had for several years, and I was determined to pursue it by the end of the calendar year, which, of course, didn't happen. There is nothing like "surprise graduate school" and three children to take all of your free time away. Alas, that's a story for another time.

Allowing yourself to live your life has ups and downs, but it's worth it. All the hours of hard work you put into pursuing your goals pay off in the future. That's the part no one sees. The magic behind the scenes is a lot of blood, sweat, and tears. Your friends and family mostly only see the results of your efforts, so pursue your dreams for yourself and not for anyone else. Work hard to make yourself proud, and don't be afraid to encourage others. That's how you get your team. Make lots of friends during your journey and maintain your sanity.

SWEET INDULGENCE

There are many flavors of romance out there, and it's up to you to experience them and choose your favorite. The first time you fall in love is unforgettable, like a monster ice cream sundae with rainbow sprinkles. You have the butterflies and the excitement that you can't contain. You experience pure enthusiasm and bliss. You start to dress a little differently, put on more makeup/cologne, pay special attention to your hair, say stupid things, and trip over yourself when "the one" is around. It's one of the best parts of being young, especially if it happens before you're out of the house alone. The first time you go through a breakup is earth-shattering like you just dropped your jumbo ice cream cone in the sand on a hot sunny day. Hopefully, it teaches you something.

I'm a firm believer that you don't truly learn these valuable life lessons until you go through hell a few times, so pack your suitcase and get it over with when you're young. That's what I tell all friends with young teenagers. Teach her to be innovative and let her get broken the first time while she's still at home. Breakups have been some of the most significant growth experiences for many people. After my first breakup, I went to college and told myself I would be strong and never need a man to care for me. I would learn to make money so I wouldn't depend on anyone.

Then, I dated my best friend for seven years. We enjoyed many great experiences together and were almost married, but I knew we had different life goals and desires. During our seven beautiful years, I was laid off from work for the first time, drove in another country for the first time, adopted my first dog, got into the bad habit of eating late, watched way too much TV, stopped loving myself, and experienced the world of video games. I wouldn't say I like video games; unfortunately, I could not compete with them. Gaming was more essential and addicting than the woman he thought he would spend the rest of his life with. This relationship taught me so many valuable lessons, and after we broke up, I gave away my television and started reading more. I read over 200 books the first year while I was single.

Breakups are scary! Your whole life changes! We're all lulled into this false sense of security in relationships, that things will always be unique, that we will grow together, and that people change. We think we'll never change jobs or get fired and won't lose anyone. The only sure thing in life is change. So why not focus on learning to change gracefully, with style and class?

Change most often occurs through a response to tough times. Remember the diamonds. Taking the easy route, staying comfortable, and not taking risks is in our blood. When you think of it, everything you do is a risk. You risk staying stagnant, or you risk failure. But sometimes, a fantastic thing happens. You take a chance, and everything turns out better than you expected. You and your life become the new and improved version of the old you. Eventually, you will gaze directly into the past at those times when you felt like your stomach was a pincushion, smile, laugh, and rejoice because you sucked it up and made something of yourself.

Vanilla, Spumoni, Surfer Dude, Pothead, Tough Guy, Nice Guy, Doctors, Bad Boy, Tall, Short, Overweight, Thin, Full of Yourself, Random Dude from the Bar. You name it, I've probably had a date with one of them, and let's say there are tons of people out there who never even came close to cutting it for a second date.

Rule number one: men, never wear a wrinkled brown t-shirt on a first date.

Rule number two: never get so drunk you don't know what's happening with the world. Be yourself, flash a smile now and again, brush your hair and teeth, and, for heaven's sake, don't smell like a three-week-old frat house laundry pile after spring break.

One of my favorite things to ask new friends is: what's the worst date you've ever been on?

Here's where I'll share some of mine just for laughs.

The Dentist- This is one of my absolute favorite date-fails. So I'm out to dinner with this dentist on the beach in Southern California, and we're talking, having a great time bringing up the science undergraduate glory days, or nightmares, depending on how positive you're feeling. The guy proceeds to tell me that I'm the most brilliant blonde woman he's ever met in his life. Being the diplomatic woman I am, I brushed it aside and made a mental note to make a beeline for the door after dinner.

I Can't Keep it in My Pants Guy- After several trials of online dating, I became thoroughly convinced that people only use these apps for "hooker-less dial-a-booty services." Some people form relationships via online dating but are few and far between. Online dates often go like this: 1. Coffee, 2. Guy tells you he wants a long-term committed relationship, 3. The guy asks you to sleep without knowing your last name. In what universe are those even remotely acceptable people? **Hooking up with someone is not dating.** It's not even love. It's lust! Do you want to spend the rest of your life with someone who doesn't care enough about getting to know you, your likes, interests, dreams, and desires? I sure as hell didn't! No, thank you, gentlemen! **News flash:** most women don't find it appealing when men update them on the state of their secondary "little brain" on date number one.

The Dreamer and Doer- I've met many people who enjoy discussing the bigger picture. There are a lot of fellow hustlers on the West Coast, and I'm privileged to call some of them my friends. Everyone needs friends who work their butts off to accomplish dreams most other people only imagine. They make and execute their plan no matter how much pain is involved. They get up every day before the crack of dawn while working on their dreams to live the life they want, whether traveling, freedom, financial success, fame, or whatever else they want to achieve with their time here. It takes a lot of hustling to form a dream team. Something I'm privileged to share with my husband.

The Ghost- Have you ever been ghosted? You've made plans with someone, and you don't receive so much as a "I don't want to continue talking to you again" text message. In this instance, you should treat others how you want to be treated. Make up your mind, listen to your heart, and then, with the decency of a kind human being, send a little note. Tell the person to thank you for enjoying time with me, but I have decided not to date you again. Be respectful to others.

If you've read this far, I encourage you to share your worst date story! Please keep it anonymous on the person's end you had a date with. We're all classy and sophisticated people here; let's not throw anyone under the bus. We all have bad days, and we all make mistakes.

EMOTIONALLY DETACHED

I'm writing this to help others in a similar situation. It's easy to start feeling like a terrible person for not getting excited about babies. Tiny humans are miracles in the flesh, brand-new souls incarnate, and you're supposed to be thrilled about these things. When my niece was born, I confided in my mother that I didn't feel excited, which genuinely bothered me. Today, I'm proud to say that I love every one of my nieces and admire their beautiful personalities. My mother reminded me of a time when my adopted grandpa passed away, and I barely took a moment to mourn. I acknowledged that I should be sad but then went about my business.

I deeply regret that I don't always allow myself to express emotions like others do, as it makes me feel out of control. Don't get me wrong; I have empathy and feelings but only sometimes show them what people expect. The older I get, the more I realize this is okay. It's essential to recognize that everyone processes emotions differently, and it's vital to make an effort to show up for those you love, even if it doesn't always look the same as how others express their feelings.

As we age, we gradually transition into new phases of our lives, forming our own paths and building our families. This transformation is not immediate; it happens slowly as we evolve into the individuals we are meant to become.

Mahatma Gandhi captured this journey eloquently with his words, "Be the change you wish to see in the world."

Even if your younger years didn't unfold as you envisioned, it's crucial to keep striving toward your goals and aspirations. The journey of self-improvement and personal fulfillment is ongoing and requires persistent effort and dedication.

Recently, I came across an intriguing reflection on the story of Lot's wife from the Bible (Genesis 19). Looking back to her past, she turned into a pillar of salt. This powerful imagery may symbolize the importance of looking forward rather than dwelling on the past. It suggests that to move towards a better future; we must focus on new opportunities and follow the plans. Dwelling on past regrets can hinder our progress, whereas embracing the future with optimism and resilience can lead to growth and transformation.

Sometimes, I think it's from growing up and having to pretend I fit in when I went to school with the other people following the blind masses. The thing is, sheep don't realize they're being sheep and unthinkingly following instructions. Don't get me wrong, I appreciated school and church as a kid and have since grown into a very spiritual woman who asks detailed questions about everything. In the formal sense of the word, I don't consider myself religious, although I consider myself a woman of strong faith. I enjoy a particular verse in the Bible, and perhaps not so coincidentally, it's repeated in many self-help and holy books worldwide. I've studied the Bible more than any other religious book, so I'll quote **Hebrews 11:1: "Faith is being sure of what you hope for and certain of what you do not see."** As I write this, I have faith that I will be able to love my future husband and children someday and that I need to start by loving myself more.

Interesting fact: as a woman, you carry your unborn children with you from birth because you are born with all the eggs you will produce in your lifetime, and that, my friends, is a beautiful thing. Just take some time to let that sink in. I just spent 15 minutes thinking about it, which made me feel hopeful about my future. Right now, I am taking the time to love myself more so that I can love others more deeply. That is half of the battle.

Your mind can play sick, twisted tricks on you, and I'm admitting these things to you, reader, so that you can know you're not alone and to show you that there is hope for you, too. Mastering your thoughts is one hell of a skill to learn. It also takes a lot of practice; don't give up.

FAMILY FORESTS

Even though this is the 21st century, people still like to complain about blended families. When I was a kid growing up with five siblings from two sets of parents, I thought it was the best thing in the world. I had three big brothers and two big sisters, whom I adored. Not everyone felt the same way. We can learn a lot from kids. They haven't become judgmental assholes like the rest of us. They love unconditionally. When things went wrong, I could always count on my siblings to advise me because they'd been there and done that. They have inspired me to try many new adventures over the years and have pushed me to follow my dreams, to work hard, and to play even harder.

My goal was to find a forever partner, someone I could navigate life's journey with and share in many adventures.

Love is exciting; sometimes, it leads you down paths you may least expect. While it is essential to remember your family's concerns about love and who you're supposed to be with, it's important to remember that you're the one who has to live with that particular person for better or worse. You and only you, not your family, have to live with that person for the remainder of your life.

Remember, **no one is perfect**. For half of the days of my life, I feel like I don't even remotely have my shit together. I'm over here refusing to wear my glasses, pretending I don't have gray hairs, and missing giant black hairs in the middle of my forehead.

I was very excited about having a significant other again, so they would let me know when I looked like some hairy mythological creature from the netherworld. On second thought, my new magnifying mirror has helped out a lot.

Just because you love someone doesn't mean they are the right person for you. Do some soul-searching and ask yourself whether or not you're living a healthy relationship. Tell your partner what you want. I believe that one of the best parts of a good relationship is when you and your significant other can be two completely different individuals with various passions but come together and enjoy the hell out of life without each losing your uniqueness and individuality.

Remember to tell them how much they mean to you. If age teaches you anything, you never know when your last day will be or when things will change. Enjoy every moment of life that you can because it will change and then change again like crazy. You can go from living a life you hate to living a life you love in months or even days.

You can move across the country, across the world, you can get a new home, and you can be homeless. **Life is full of possibilities! Don't let anyone convince you otherwise.** Yes, life gets freaky-scary, and you often have no earthly idea what you're doing, who you are, or even what you're good at. Keep on going, keep on coming up with ideas, and keep on pursuing your dreams. It only takes one small step at a time to make that difference in your life.

A REVELATION CALLS

I spent many years trying to find myself, and one day, I finally realized that none of us find ourselves, it's a journey. We all need to focus on creating ourselves with daily change.

Every one of us is a perception of our imagination. Want to be a different person? Ideas become things; thoughts become tangible in our lives. So many poor souls have never realized that. One of the best ways to stay in debt is to focus on what you lack in your life. One of the best ways to stay single is to focus on what you think you don't have. Learn to live and never give up. Things then miraculously fall into place, and by miraculously falling into place, I mean you have to put yourself out there and enjoy some Awkward Romance. Step out of your comfort zone! Go all in with a chance of losing or an even bigger chance of winning!

Most self-help books I've read, over 200 by now, mention writing down things about your childhood to help you discover your goals. I did that and came up with a few themes from childhood. First, I realized I had always liked speaking or singing in front of others. Something I'd been doing since I could legitimately sing, "All I want for Christmas is my Two Front Teeth, "with the awkward toothless lisp from missing my front teeth. Another noteworthy confession would be that I had never liked just doing whatever everyone else did in school. I used to get in trouble for finishing my homework during class and not paying attention, and I'm pretty sure my Grandma thought my school didn't give homework when I was a kid. In reality, it was all done because I hated working on school work at home and could experience absolute freedom. That has been an overwhelmingly important aspect of every job I've chosen, every study I've done, and most of my life. I learned that I value my time, love working hard on things I enjoy, and hate having a regular job and accepting the status quo.

My motto in life was always that if "name any person" can do it, then why can't I? Sometimes, that doesn't get you far because people don't believe in your crazy ideas. You start on a new adventure and work your ass off to make a business work, and all they can think about is you starving to death and not being able to afford a pair of shoes and having to turn into a shoeless person playing music on the street to pay your electric bill. Welcome to the world of negative thoughts; don't let those creep up on you. One of my favorite experiences with a family member was telling them I always felt I would be highly successful. The wonderful relative then proceeded to ask me if I was mentally ill and experiencing "delusions of grandeur." Classy!

If there's one thing I've learned from this over the years, it is to stop listening to all the advice you get from other people. You never have to be totally on your own and start busking, even though it often seems like an excellent idea except for the thought of ending up in a murder mystery episode on the Investigative Discovery channel, or your mom finding out. To clear this up for all those of you who find yourself wondering. The answer is a hard NO. I've never had to sleep on the street and have never even had to consider it an option. It doesn't happen, but you keep that in your mind as an option should all hell break loose.

LOVE REDISCOVERED

One never knows when they will find love. It just sneaks up on you like Cupid shooting you with his bow in the behind while you're not paying attention. It's funny how things happen that never in your wildest dreams could you imagine. When you open your heart up to love, you make countless friends along the way. When you open your life up to new experiences, sometimes the new friends you make along the way often become more like family. The only reason you're ever disappointed is when you allow yourself to see disappointment. You find good things when you look for good things and put out good things. Many people say they want to love, but are they truly willing to sacrifice what it takes to be in a relationship? I spent several years being single by choice because I hadn't found anyone who fit the standards I made for myself.

Then, when you approach 30 people, they ask you the dreaded: "Why does a pretty girl like yourself not have a boyfriend?" The older men you run into tell you you have a lucky boyfriend. You tell them you're single, and they ask how. Then, all of a sudden, you go through a phase where you think something is most definitely wrong with you because you're still single and close to 30. You start to question the meaning of life; panic pours through your mind like a disgusting green ooze. It starts to seem like working, paying taxes, eating lettuce, gaining emotional baggage, and dying are the only things you're suitable for as a human for a while until you snap out of it and realize that sitting back and letting life beat you down isn't the answer to living a fulfilling life. It's been my experience that it is time for a change when you start feeling this way. It doesn't have to be a significant change. Attending an event twice a month, getting a new haircut, taking a day off, wearing red lipstick, or anything you need to get out of that funk. You know, like jumping out of an airplane on a random Wednesday morning for no reason other than you want to do so. I did that. It was a blast; no regrets.

One particular Thursday night in April, I got a feeling in my gut that I would have a date on Friday night, so I made reservations for two at a restaurant and planned to ask someone to go out with me the next day, whomever I ran into. It was my only day off for the week, so I had a lot of errands to run. I ran 5 miles on the trail and donated blood. By the time 7 pm rolled around, I was too tired to go out for dinner 10 miles away, so I decided to go to the wine bar near home for flourless chocolate cake and a glass of cabernet. While sitting at the bar, I got a text message from a guy I had met at a business networking event months ago asking me to go out for a drink with him. We enjoyed a splendid evening full of laughs and stories. Then the night was over, and I never heard from him again. Does that sound like some of your dates? Who cares? I didn't have to sit at home watching TV alone in my pajamas. Life is about having fun until the right person for you comes along. Keep your chin up and your head held high. You got this!

NAVIGATING
THE DIVIDE

I was inspired to write this book for many reasons. Still, the primary motivation was the vast number of gorgeous but cynical, well-educated, sometimes nerdy, single women I have the pleasure of knowing and hearing profoundly negative remarks from regarding dating or life in general. So now I'm calling you out for all the complaining because complaining doesn't change anything. The band Nazareth put it quite well when they sang, "Love Hurts, Love scars, Love wounds and marks Any heart not tough or strong enough To take a lot of pain, take a lot of pain Love is like a cloud, it holds a lot of rain, Love hurts." It's time for us to rise to the occasion and accept that nothing good in life comes easy; you must work for it. You have to wake up early and pound the pavement for anything you truly desire, especially when dating once you've become an adult with responsibilities and had a few bad relationships. The only person you can change in life is you. You can't change other people; frankly, if you try to change them, you will end up sorely disappointed, a few dollars short, and possibly in a bit of a tizzy. For those unfamiliar with pandemonium, it means a restless or nervous state.

When we first fall in love as children, we don't have the

responsibilities and defined lives of adulthood. We haven't given up our sense of freedom and adventure or forgotten how to think outside the box. Slowly, we become comfortable with our careers and our definition of who we are in relation to what we do. Ask any adult to tell you about him or herself, and they will most likely tell you what they do for a living. So often, we start to check the boxes society has to define our lives—school, marriage, house, kids, 401k. We, as humans, are so much more than our careers. We go from childhood where we say things like, "I love the color red, I have a best friend named Sally, and the monkey bars are fun." To say, "I'm an overweight "insert job here" from who knows where "insert complaint here."" We get comfortable. The thought of compromising for another human being suddenly feels out of the question.

Why should I be the one to change? Some of us wait for a significant other to save us and improve our lives. We may even have the audacity to think that a successful individual who has worked hard for the lifestyle that they have will choose us, like a fairy tale. One moment, sitting on the couch in our living room that hasn't been cleaned in months, binge-watching Netflix and pounding back glasses of wine or beer with a side of chocolate ice cream and yesterday's cold pizza, wearing sweatpants, having not showered in two days. The next minute, "Prince Charming" swoops in and rescues us. We take monthly trips to the Bahamas, have two houses, drive expensive luxury cars, have the best wardrobe, our kids go to the best private school, speak five languages, and are miraculously fit and in good shape. I'm not saying that doesn't happen sometimes, but my friend, the odds are against you.

The sweet spot for finding love is slowly peeling away those cynical, eye-watering, stinky onion layers and learning to see the world with a childlike sense of wonder. Remember when you didn't just like someone and spend time with them because you wanted something from them when you were a kid? You just wanted to play. You didn't have ulterior motives like getting married, having babies, buying houses, and starting 401k. Those things are beautiful parts of adult life, but maybe the answer lies somewhere in between. Learning to be with someone just because you enjoy his or her company may be an excellent place to start. I firmly believe in the K.I.S.S. principle (Keep it simple, stupid). For my nerdy friends, you can also think of Occam's razor or the "law of parsimony." This law states that when there is more than one possible answer to a problem, choose the one that makes the least assumptions or the Keep It Simple Stupid method. The most crucial phrase in the law is the part about making the least assumptions.

Some of the assumptions we tend to make when dating include but are not limited to the following:

- **We went out twice, and I think we will get married now because he/she is terrific.** Don't even do that to yourself! Good relationships take time to cultivate, just like tending to a garden. You need some sunshine, some water, and a lot of love. You deserve to be courted and cherished and have someone care enough about you to take time and put effort into having a relationship with you. They want to see you, they want to spend time with you, and they want to be around you.

- **They didn't text me all week and must no longer be interested.**

- **He/she got arrested recently, but I will hide that from my family because they've changed.** This one I'm calling big bullshit on! People make mistakes, but they establish unhealthy patterns, too! Everyone does it! Some of us are fat! Some of us are bitchy! Some of us are convicts! Some of us do drugs! Some of us don't listen! When you see these big bright red flags waving in your face, then you need to take a step back and evaluate things! Evaluate the hell out of the situation, and ask for advice from a trusted friend. Whatever you do! Do not keep these things a secret. Eventually, everyone will discover them. Save yourself the embarrassment. If you can't tell your loved ones about your current date's past or present, you must think before taking another step. Promise me you will not ignore the red flags! Especially when someone has a "record" of doing stupid things repeatedly. Step back and evaluate how you want to deal with this situation. Are you willing to live with this person at their worst? Because when you sign the dotted line, you're supposed to be in it for the long haul.

- **Naming all of our future children on date three isn't crazy.**

- **You think that the person you're seeing isn't seeing someone else.** Almost everyone has done that at some point or another. That's why when you start to get serious about them, you must talk about dating other people. Relationships take commitment to one another, and if you never get to the point of asking this question, move on already, for heaven's sake! If you don't feel guilty about going out with another person when you have met someone you genuinely care about, then perhaps they aren't the one.

Suppose you are one of those cynical, well-educated women. You better check yourself before you wreck yourself. The first step is to stop making assumptions because those can go from tiny to astronomical mistakes in a heartbeat. Another critical point is recognizing that you are not and will never be perfect. In real life, things don't always happen as planned. Take some time to learn how to let go and let live. I know, I'm a type A individual in some ways. Have you ever see Desperate Housewives? Well, a character on that show named Bree Vandecamp lets her neighbors think she's perfect in every way. There is never a stray hair on her head. Then she ends up having to cover up that her son committed vehicular homicide, her daughter gets pregnant, and her husband leaves her. Everyone resents Bree, but then she has a meltdown and reinvents herself with a new life, just like people's social media lives. Everything looks fantastic in the pictures, but what is behind the scenes counts the most.

The most crucial step in really finding love is mastering the art of self-love first. I know, I know, everyone says that's the case, but how are you supposed to do that when you're wallowing in self-pity about being single and not knowing what to do? No, there's nothing wrong with you. Trust me. We've all heard we're supposed to work on ourselves, and you're thinking how I did in varying degrees of profanities smothered with a bit of salt to rub in the wounds. Am I right?

Here's the deal. Nothing good happens overnight. This is something you have to work on slowly. Consider allowing room in your budget to go to that yoga class you love once a week. If you go out to eat often, one way to cut costs is to go out for an appetizer and drink or to forgo dining out altogether. Try things that scare you at least once a week. Something you've never done before or something that you'd like to try. Something you used to enjoy regularly. Use your imagination.

For example, I started working with a business and success coach this week. I've been talking about making changes in my life, and I wasn't making them fast enough, so I'm moving onward and upward from here. I used to take a PowerPoint presentation along with job interviews with me that had a graph on it, a highly scientific chart. It featured a red line with an arrow pointing in an upward-sloping direction to the right with no axis descriptions whatsoever, thus illustrating my growth strategy. So, it finally seemed time to get my butt in gear and make something happen. Here goes nothing!

EQUILIBRIUM

For many years, when crazy things happened, I have always asked myself, "What is my purpose?" I never knew what I was supposed to do, who I was supposed to be, or why I never felt like I fit in with others. I started working at age 14 because that was what you were supposed to do. Still, unlike my other classmates, I squirreled it away so I wouldn't be in so much debt after college. I worked this way for thirteen more years, moved across a continent, almost got married, and finally realized that I was working away from the best and most carefree part of my life without a purpose and no concrete plans. Growing up, I never learned about setting goals or making plans and why they were important. But I did know that the other kids in school lived in much nicer houses than I did and went on way better vacations with their families to faraway exotic places. On the other hand, I didn't try sushi until 8th grade and spent most of my childhood working on construction projects with my father.

There was a time in my early 20s when I resented how I grew up. I was embarrassed and ashamed to introduce them to my friends' parents, who were attorneys, entrepreneurs, and CFOs. As I've grown older, I've also appreciated everything I've learned that most women have never heard of. If there is a plumbing issue at 3 am at my house, I can handle it! If my parents taught me anything, it was the value of hard work and determination. They provided a wonderful childhood, which I appreciate as I grow older. They are still working hard. And it is their hard work that prompted me to speak with all those attorneys, entrepreneurs, and CFOs about what they did to get where they were. The second best thing my parents taught me was that asking people who know more than you questions is what it takes to be successful. The truth is I have no reason to complain about my childhood. I never went hungry and always had a roof over my head. That's how I became addicted to working all the time because I wanted to get ahead in life. By the time I reached the age of 26, I realized that working hard is great, but working smart and with a purpose is what gets you ahead in life. I was working away the best years of my life when I should have also taken time to connect with people I cared about.

Establishing a work-life balance is one of the most critical aspects of renewing your dating life. For those who don't know what that means, it's taking time for yourself. No one can sustain himself or herself working tirelessly day and night with no breaks. You are your most prominent advocate; don't let anyone take away that right. Sometimes, however, you may find yourself in a situation where life throws you some plot twists, and you don't work that many hours, but in reality, it feels like forever. Perhaps you're in the wrong place. Henceforth, I'm allowing you to get your hands dirty and try new things. New adventures are less scary when you plan, even just a little.

I'd also be a hypocrite if I didn't tell you right off the bat that this is the thing I struggle with the most in my life. Instead, I'd work my booty off every day rather than take time to establish and maintain worthwhile relationships. There is no shame in my game. This is something that I struggle with daily. Then, I find myself thinking about starting another dead-end job that would pay well. I get sad about doing something I hate for someone I don't care about in one bit for a paycheck that will never even get me ahead. I don't want to work on someone else's dream; I want to work on mine. The biggest thing I've discovered by writing this book is that it could be a better use of time to do something that helps you step closer to accomplishing your goals. You sit there feeling sad, punching the clock again, hating your life and everything, and feeling like you need some sleep. I've been there a million times. I've only taken one to two days off a month for the past year. However, I'm still getting this information out to all of you because something inside me said my story could encourage others to keep going, dreaming, and pursuing their personal goals and passions.

I've done everything wrong regarding relationships in the past. I used to blame that on never really seeing a good relationship as a kid. I ran away when I was fighting with significant others and told them I never wanted to see their face again. I've yelled, and I've never taken the time to truly appreciate the good things in life. Never again. When you care about someone, tell them. Please don't keep it a secret. If they reject you, then that is on them, and you are no worse off than you were before you told them how you felt.

One thing that changed my life was deciding to take full responsibility for everything that happened. Even down to the nitty-gritty details. **As Earnest Nightengale eloquently said, "We're all self-made, but only the successful will admit it."** You can never fully take control of your life until you admit to yourself that all you have is "you." You are responsible for your destiny, your choices, where you live, how you dress, how you feel, and who your friends are. There's a whole world out there for you to explore until you find your specific niche, where you thrive, where you feel the most comfortable, and the thing that gives you that upper hand to be on your A-game more than you're crying alone whenever you have the chance feeling pitiful about yourself and making excuses for why you haven't done more lived more, been more. If you don't want to regret never having lived on your deathbed, you better start living RIGHT NOW. Don't you dare wait until tomorrow!

WEBSTER

Merriam-Webster's dictionary defines purpose as something set up as an object or end to be attained an intention. One of the biggest struggles we all face is determining our purpose. For some of us, our epiphany of purpose comes at an early age. For others, it takes many years to cultivate. Vast majorities of people on this planet never discover their true purpose and, on their deathbed, realize that one of their biggest regrets, other than not loving and living enough, is never realizing their potential and purpose. Life is scary, risks are inevitable, and true love never fails. Words are often cheap, so the adage, "Actions speak louder than words," exists.

I spent many years searching for that elusive thing called purpose. I read books, attended seminars, asked professionals for help, and even hired business coaches. Then, one day, I read a great **book by Napoleon Hill entitled, "Wishes Won't Bring Riches."** In summary, Napoleon says that many people search for a lifetime for their purpose and never find it. Few decide their purpose and work with it to accomplish goals and dreams that many thought impossible. Just make it up as you go along like the rest of us!

Goals are essential to set at any stage or situation in life. Scheduling time in your busy life to set goals is an excellent way to help you find your purpose or to **give the meaning of your decision**. Keep your goals organized in a small journal or notebook. Writing your thoughts down can help you establish patterns in your life and give you clues about where your strengths lie. I take a few minutes while driving to work, or as I like to call it, my private phone booth, to decide on the three most significant things I'd like to accomplish for the day. These are not long-term goals; they are the tasks you should review each evening to metaphorically pat yourself on the back for a job well done.

Here's an example of some of mine:

- Write 1,000 words for this book.
- Drink a gallon of water.
- Practice faith today.

These are not the only things I will accomplish today, but they are the most important to me this morning.

These will help me achieve my long-term goals for the year:

- Publishing a book.
- Fitting into my high school booty shorts.
- Creating a new business for myself that uses all or more of my skill sets.

Take some time today to shortlist things you would like to accomplish this year or this quarter. Keep in mind that this does not need to be too detailed. One of the best things to remember is to think small. Many small tasks and accomplishments make for a lot of progress. Stay calm when looking at all the long-term goals; break them up and come closer to your goals every day. You are the author of your destiny.

After many sleepless nights of soul-searching misery and pain when your loving -Insert the name of caring relative here- sends you yet another relationship and dating advice book which has absolutely no hints of anything in it that doesn't make you feel like crying and running away forever and burying your head under a rock. Then you finally say fuck it and use them all to start your fires when you go camping because you intuitively know you're going to be ok if you just take some time for yourself and stop working seven days a week. Go with your gut and live, but live with a purpose.

Don't attend events solely because you're invited. Only volunteer for something you're passionate about. **Learn how to say no and how to stand up for yourself. Learn what you do and do not like.** Then, do what you enjoy because, for heaven's sake, life is so short that by the time you realize what's happening, you are pushing 30 and still single, writing a book at the library in a fancy dress before night school, and debating whether or not you can afford to buy a coffee at the coffee shop for the night, worried about every little thing on your to-do list. At the same time, thoughts keep racing in your head. You start to think you're crazy until you talk to other people who have experienced the same situation and finally just sit back, take a sip of that overpriced coffee, and say enough is enough. I will follow my passions, live the life I've imagined, and become the @CEOLivingtheDream because I want to inspire other people to live life truly and not simply go through the motions of the script before us.

What is the difference between an amateur and a professional musician? The answer is the same thing as what makes a fulfilled person and a person who lives a life of quiet desperation. An accomplished musician doesn't just play the notes written on the page. They interpret them, add to them, change them all of a sudden, and emphasize the tone of the music. The piece goes from loud to soft to very quiet, almost inaudible. You can feel the passion flowing from their skilled hands and voices and understand that they've practiced countless hours to achieve perfection. Ergo, you can only go through life and have a wild adventure with a bit of work. But it's worth it. Like a skilled musician, you learn to "feel the music." Don't just go through life; embrace it, make your mark, and then reap the benefits of blessing others with your talents and spirit. Touch people's lives. Like a good musician, remove yourself from the equation and focus on making the art. Understand how your actions make you feel; then focus on following what makes you feel on point! Understand what propels you out of bed every morning, ready to rock the world. Don't just take it from me; do it yourself. You'll be surprised just how far your dreams, ambitions, a bit of homework, and gut feelings will take you.

THE GENESIS

T he man I had been searching for was finally in my circle. As I write this, I'm confident that the man of my dreams is already in my life. Let me tell you the short version. It was a Hollywood movie plot in real life. At the beginning of January, I decided it was about time to attend Toastmasters meetings because I was determined to become a motivational speaker. I love speaking and inspiring people. Toastmasters, week number two, and one of the girls gets up and gives her presentation on the best dating apps, which ones to use, and what to avoid. She recommended Ok-Cupid, which I thought was for old people. Prepare yourself for a bit of hypocrisy in the following story. Hey, you live and learn. I was recently single and not in any mood to date whatsoever. My broken heart was still healing, and I needed to have my solo- adventure before getting into a relationship again. You know, when you hear the couple who says you are instantly attracted. I never believed that kind of attraction existed, even in my wildest dreams. It seemed too far-fetched to be true.

On that fateful day, I had a date with destiny. I was too stubborn to realize that at first. My future husband and I spent time together hiking, working out, and cooking several times before I opened my heart to dating again. I moved to California during a tumultuous time in my life. I had gone through a breakup after dating for almost eight years. That's longer than many marriages last. I must have been blind not to realize who was next to me. The person I had been looking for, my husband, was already in my life. We enjoyed spending time together, with lots of laughs, and we understood each other from the moment we met. We were great friends.

On our second date, we met to go jogging. I had a super sexy asthma attack, was unable to breathe, and was coughing up who knows what afterward for hours. Attractive; I know. This guy called me again the next day. Fireworks were going off all around me. I am nearly incapable of realizing when a man is flirting with me. That is not one of my strong suits. Don't be afraid to admit you're oblivious to flirting. Many women feel this way because, from a young age, we program ourselves to tune men out. After all, catcalling is a real issue for many women. I admit that I am bad at knowing when men are flirting with me and when they like me.

The more I reflect on my journey, the more I realize there were many missed opportunities for love. I never took the time to appreciate love. I didn't know how to love or understand what it meant to love someone. Looking back, I would tell my younger self to go out with more men, especially in high school. It's essential to establish the ability to learn about healthy relationships while you still have some guidance from your family and a set schedule. Let your heart get broken for the first time before you start working full-time and don't have anyone around to support you. We met for a second date to enjoy some Syrian food where I was the sluttiest girl in the restaurant because I had on a knee length shift dress, not a burka.

Since this chapter is entitled "The End," I wrote it at the very last second. I'm sitting in my living room in California, so excited to see the man of my dreams when he gets home from work tonight.

I'm sitting here thinking of how we'll enjoy our evening cup of tea together with our young son. We will have a wonderful life full of spending time together and going on adventures. We always have a blast doing anything and everything. I knew he was a big deal when he introduced me to his mom. In Middle-Eastern culture, if the woman you like meets your mother, you're interested in getting married. Before we married, I had no idea about this custom. Would our relationship work out at first? No! But I was damn sure we were going to enjoy the journey because it had been life-changing. When my mother-in-law asked my parents if we could get married, they had no idea what she meant. The man's father (or mom in our case), in Syrian culture, is the one who asks the bride's parents if they can be married.

I've always been an extremely stubborn woman, and admittedly, I never have felt pretty enough, dainty enough, smart enough, or fit enough for a member of the opposite sex to find me attractive. That doesn't mean that they do not see me as beautiful; when a man told me in the past that I looked like a goddess, I thought they were joking because there was no way anyone would find me attractive. Growing up, I always towered above the other ladies and was much stronger than them by far; I was and still am taller than the average man. After many years of following the self-doubt spiral into oblivion, I decided to start finding myself attractive, and it didn't matter what other people thought of me. I decided to eat healthy because it made me feel good and more energetic. I decided to take up hiking and trail running because it made me feel powerful. I decided to take time every morning to do my hair and makeup because it made me feel like I, in some small way, had my shit together. I also decided to start wearing high heels again because they made me feel like a million bucks.

It's always possible to turn things around. Do them yourself, and people will notice you becoming more confident and happy. Keep it up long enough, and you may even inspire that other person you once were to start living their dreams. You may even wake up one day and realize that you are special and an invaluable asset to the world. You are a hero, a pioneer, and a badass in whatever you choose to do!

Life is a beautiful mess, but it's yours to live nonetheless. Don't let anyone make the important decisions in life for you. That task is up to you. Occasional stormy seas shouldn't ruin life's voyage. Adventure is not about the destination; it's the journey. Then, it's the destination and a new journey.

ABOUT THE AUTHOR

Emily Rassam wears many hats - as a motivational speaker, author, entrepreneur, former scientist (on the road to recovery), a self-proclaimed nerdy badass woman, and a dedicated wife and mom. She enjoys long and occasionally intense uphill "walks" along the beach or mountain trail. Recognized for her outspoken nature and confidence, Emily breaks the rules to inspire others to embrace their envisioned lives, crediting her resilience to faith, loved ones, and her amazing husband, Abe.

https://x.com/theemilyrassam

https://www.facebook.com/iloveemilyamen

http://eepurl.com/iWulok

EPILOGUE

As you reach the final pages of "Awkward Romance: A Nerdy Girl's Dating Manifesto," I want to leave you with one last thought. The journey of love, life, and self-discovery is never truly over. It's a continuous adventure filled with new challenges, unexpected joys, and moments of growth.

When I began writing this book, I was looking for answers like many of you. I wanted to make sense of the awkwardness, doubts, and sometimes hilarious missteps that come with navigating relationships. But along the way, I realized something profound: there is no one-size-fits-all solution to love, no perfect formula or magic trick that will guarantee you a smooth ride. And that's okay.

I've learned that the awkwardness and uncertainty are not just obstacles to overcome—they make the journey beautiful. They are the moments that shape us, teach us, and ultimately lead us to where we need to be. In those awkward moments, we find our true selves.

So, if there's one message I hope you take away from this book, it's this: embrace the awkwardness. Lean into the quirks that make you who you are. Don't be afraid to take risks, make mistakes, and laugh at yourself. In doing so, you open yourself to the kind of love and life that are uniquely yours.

Remember, the journey doesn't end here. Whether you're just starting out on your romantic path or you've been traveling it for a while, there's always more to discover, more to learn, and more to love. Keep going, keep growing, and most importantly, keep being your wonderfully awkward self.

Thank you for sharing this journey with me. I hope these pages have brought you a smile, comfort, and maybe even a new perspective on love. Here's to the next chapter of your story—may it be filled with laughter, love, and awkward adventures.

With all my heart,

Emily Rassam

AFTERWORD

As I wrap up this journey of "Awkward Romance," I reflect on the incredible adventure it has been—from the initial spark of inspiration to the many late nights spent writing and revising. This book is more than just a collection of stories and advice; it's a piece of my heart, and I'm so grateful to have shared it with you.

When I first set out to write this book, I aimed to capture the ups and downs of dating as a nerdy girl, embrace the awkwardness, and turn it into something beautiful. Along the way, I've learned so much—not just about relationships but about myself and the importance of self-acceptance, courage, and perseverance.

Writing this book has been an emotional rollercoaster, filled with moments of doubt and exhilaration. But knowing that it might resonate with others who have felt the same way made every challenge worthwhile. This journey succeeds if even one reader finds comfort, laughter, or a sense of connection in these pages.

I want to thank everyone who supported me through this process —my family, friends, beta readers, and all of you who have followed along. Your encouragement has been my fuel, and your belief in this project has kept me going.

As you close this book, I hope you take the reminder that it's okay to be awkward, embrace your quirks, and pursue love and happiness in your own unique way. Life is full of unexpected twists and turns; sometimes, the most awkward moments lead to the most incredible adventures.

Thank you for being part of this journey with me. Here's to many more adventures on the page and in life.

Go Have Some Fun,

Emily Rassam

Made in the USA
Columbia, SC
07 February 2025

52736458R00046